Eloise Visits
the Zoo

KAY THOMPSON'S ELOISE

Eloise Visits the Zoo

STORY BY **Lisa McClatchy**

ILLUSTRATED BY **Tammie Lyon**

Ready-to-Read

Aladdin

NEW YORK · LONDON · TORONTO · SYDNEY

ALADDIN PAPERBACKS
An imprint of Simon & Schuster Children's Publishing Division
1230 Avenue of the Americas, New York, NY 10020
Copyright © 2009 by the Estate of Kay Thompson
"Eloise" and related marks are trademarks of the Estate of Kay Thompson.
All rights reserved, including the right of reproduction in whole or in part in any form.
ALADDIN PAPERBACKS and related logo and READY-TO-READ are registered
trademarks of Simon & Schuster, Inc.
The text of this book was set in Century Old Style.
Manufactured in the United States of America
First Aladdin Paperbacks edition May 2009
6 8 10 9 7 5
Cataloging-in-Publication Data is on file with the Library of Congress.
ISBN: 978-1-4169-8642-3
0613 LAK

My name is Eloise.
I am a city child.

I am also an animal lover.
I love Weenie, my dog.

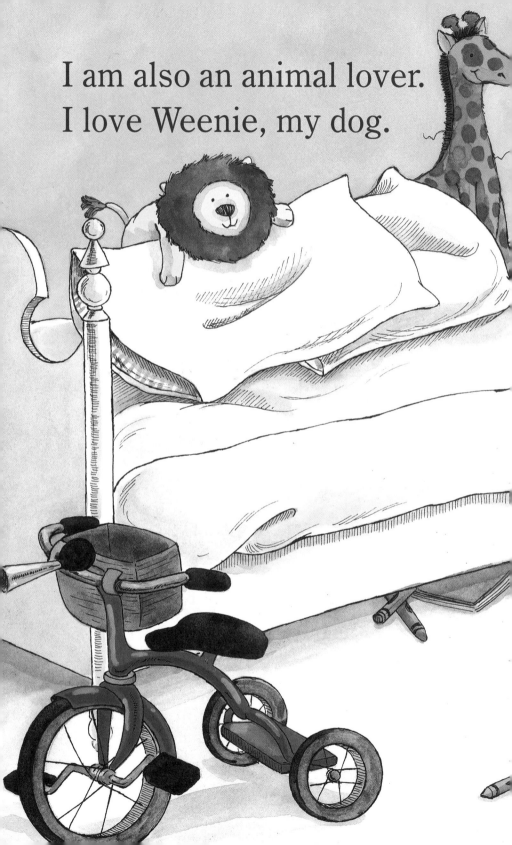

I love Skipperdee, my turtle.

And I love, love, love
going to the zoo!

"It is summertime!"
I say to Nanny.

The perfect time
for going to the zoo.

Nanny and I wear
our safari best.

We wear our safari hats.
And our safari vests.

And, of course, we bring
our safari camera
and our binoculars.

There is so much
to see at the zoo!

"To Africa first, Nanny," I say.
Nanny and I study the
lowland gorillas.

We say hello back
to the lions.

The giraffe tries
to lick my hand.
"No, no, no, Eloise!"
says Nanny.

Oh, I love, love, love
giraffes!

"To Australia now, Nanny,"
I say.
Nanny and I take pictures
of the kangaroos.

We sketch the koalas in
their eucalyptus trees

"Here, Nanny," I say.
"Would you like to
feed the lorries too?"

"No, no, no, Eloise!"
says Nanny.

Oh, I love,
love, love
lorries.

"To North America!"
I yell to Nanny.
We howl along with
the gray wolves.

We search for the black bear.

We visit the petting zoo.
"May I take a billy goat
home, Nanny?" I ask.

"No, no, no, Eloise!"
Nanny says.
Oh, I love, love, love
billy goats.

"To the nursery last,"
I say to Nanny.
We sing to the baby
chimpanzee.

We whisper hello to
the sleeping wombat.

A volunteer asks Nanny if we would like to see the new baby elephant.

"Oh, yes!" Nanny and
I say together.

Oh, I love, love, love
the zoo!